Little Louis
Takes Off

For my parents
and
in memory of my grandfather,
Oscar Morison, an early aviator

SIMON AND SCHUSTER

First published in Great Britain in 2007 by Simon & Schuster UK Ltd

Africa House, 64-78 Kingsway, London WC2B 6AH

A CBS COMPANY

Book designed by Genevieve Webster
The text for this book is set in Bodoni
The illustrations are rendered in watercolour

A CIP catalogue record for this book is available from
the British Library upon request

ISBN-10: 1-416-90435-2
ISBN-13: 9781416904359

Printed in China

1 3 5 7 9 10 8 6 4 2

Little Louis
Takes Off

Toby Morison

SIMON AND SCHUSTER
London New York Sydney

Little Louis had still not learnt to fly.

"Come on, you can do it!" cheered his brothers and sisters.

"I'm trying," he sighed.

But he just couldn't get the hang of it.

Louis always felt much more chirpy playing
hopscotch or flying his kite.

His favourite hobby of all was plane-spotting. Kitted out with his 8x30 binoculars, Louis studied the aeroplanes as they soared gracefully in the sky, and he kept a record of them all in a special spiral-bound notebook.

As winter approached, his family prepared to fly south for their holiday in the sun. Before they left, they took Louis to the airport.

"I don't want to go alone," Louis sniffled. "I want to go with you!"

"Shame you can't fly like normal birds, then," muttered his father.

"Come on, sweetie, don't flap," said his mother. "Going by plane will be very exciting, and we'll see you very soon!"

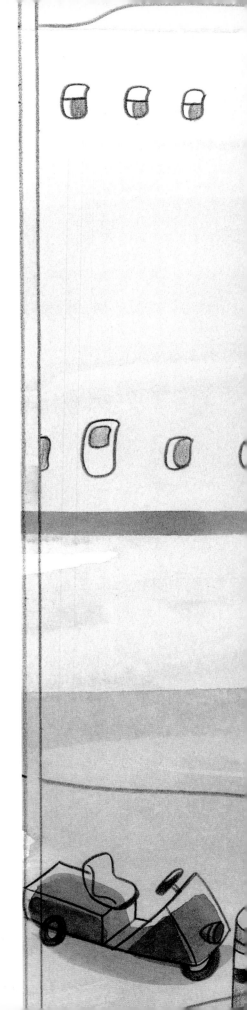

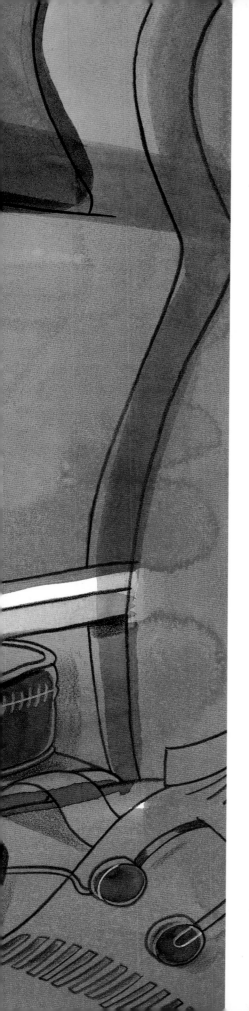

Louis still felt wobbly, but once the
plane took off he became much calmer.

He nibbled a few peanuts, then nestled
against the pillow and drifted off to sleep.
He dreamt he could fly.

When the plane landed, Louis woke
with a start. "That was a bit bumpy,"
he thought, but he was too polite to
mention it, especially as he couldn't
fly himself.

"Hello, birdie! I'm Guido," said a flamingo in a heavy accent. "I take you to hotel. Vamoose!"

When they arrived, Louis looked up at the hotel rooftop. He was tired and he missed his family. "I want my mummy," he said in a shaky voice.

"You wait long time," snorted Guido. "Too bad you no can fly." And, with that, he was gone.

LITTLE LOUIS

It was a long hop up to the rooftop for Louis' tiny legs. "Four hundred and eighty-five, four hundred and eighty-six…" he counted the steps, "…four hundred and eighty-seven!"

At last, he was there. Little Louis fell asleep straight away.

In the morning Louis woke up feeling utterly alone. First, he checked that his return plane ticket was safe.

Then he opened his airline grooming case and gave himself a good preening.

Louis picked up his binoculars and scanned the skies, looking desperately for his family. But there was no sign of them.

That night he cried himself to sleep.

The next day as he scanned the horizon, Louis spotted a penguin. It was standing alone on a rock, folding paper aeroplanes and propelling them into the air. Louis longed to join in and make a friend.

He was watching so intently that he didn't notice his precious plane ticket being picked up by the breeze... Then, just as it fluttered over the edge of the roof, it caught his eye.

Without thinking, Louis swooped after it!

Help!

He was falling…

plummeting
to the ground
in a tail-spin…

Mayday!
Mayday!

Louis
swallowed
hard...

…then suddenly he felt his wing tips lift
and he began to climb.

Louis plucked the ticket from the air
and soared into the glorious blue sky.

He was flying!

From high above, Little Louis saw the penguin!
He swooped down and landed with a bump.

"Hello!" said the penguin. "My name's
Gwynn. Flying must be thirsty work!" he added,
as he offered Louis a drink.

Louis told Gwynn all about the aeroplane, the
ticket and how much he missed his family.

"Oh, don't fret," said Gwynn kindly. "They'll
turn up soon — it's just that birds fly much more
slowly than aeroplanes. But if you ever feel lonely,
you're always welcome here."

"Thank you, Gwynn," said Louis.

"That's what friends are for!" smiled Gwynn.

Louis flew down to see Gwynn every day. They soon became the best of friends. They talked for hours about all the places they'd like to see in the world.

"But I'll never be able to go anywhere," sighed Gwynn. "You see, penguins can't fly – we're too heavy and our wings aren't big enough."

Louis felt sorry for Gwynn. He wished there was something he could do to help.

Then, one happy morning, Little Louis' family finally flew into view. He had a surprise welcome ready for them.

"Bravo to our little high-flyer!" they cried.

"I'm very proud of you," said his father, giving him a hug.

Louis' chest swelled. "Oh, it was a breeze," he said airily.

Reunited at last, the family enjoyed a wonderful holiday together. Little Louis practised doing loops and rolls, and soon he joined his brothers and sisters in aerobatic displays.

He took them all to meet Gwynn, who showed them how to make paper aeroplanes.

Time flew by, and soon the day came for Louis to say farewell to his special friend. He gave Gwynn a big hug and handed him a long envelope…

Louis' family was ready to leave.

"Now don't fly too fast," they chorused,
"it's going to be a long haul!"

But Louis had more important things on his
mind when he took to the skies...

As a plane flew past, he urgently scanned the
windows. His wings beat faster in delight
as he recognised, in seat 17E, a first-time flyer.

Gwynn grinned and waved.

Louis smiled and swooped to join his family
in formation as they headed for home.